TILLY'S PONY TAILS

Pride and Joy
the event horse

TILLY'S PONY TAILS

Pride and Joy
the event horse

PIPPA FUNNELL

Illustrated by Jennifer Miles

Orion
Children's Books

First published in Great Britain in 2010
by Orion Children's Books
a division of the Orion Publishing Group Ltd
Orion House
5 Upper St Martin's Lane
London WC2H 9EA
An Hachette UK Company

1 3 5 7 9 8 6 4 2

ISBN 978 1 4440 0081 8

Printed and bound in the UK by CPI Mackays, Chatham ME5 8TD

www.orionbooks.co.uk
www.tillysponytails.co.uk

For Primmore's Pride,
who inspired this story

One

It was early summer and the stable yard at Silver Shoe Farm was busy as usual. People trooped to and fro, carrying saddles and bridles. The sound of happy chatter filled the air as both riders and horses eagerly anticipated hacking in the countryside or a lesson in the sand school. Tilly Redbrow loved Silver Shoe Farm at this time of year.

In fact, Tilly loved everything about Silver Shoe Farm, come rain or shine. Since going there she'd learned so much. She knew all about caring for horses, about tack, mucking out and grooming. She knew the basics of how to work a horse on the flat, and her jumping had improved enormously since she'd first started.

The one thing Silver Shoe couldn't teach her, however, was how to use her special gift for communicating with horses. This came to Tilly instinctively. Ever since the dramatic rescue of her favourite horse, Magic Spirit, from the middle of the town,

she'd realised she had an unusual talent for
calming them. It had puzzled her at first,
but gradually Tilly realised she could make
use of it. From great racehorses, like Red
Admiral, to gentle ponies, like Rosie, the
strawberry roan she shared with her friend
Mia, they'd all been helped by Tilly's
instinctive understanding.

Today Tilly had no need for this talent
because Magic Spirit was completely calm.
He stood, tied up outside his stable,

enjoying a thorough grooming. His grey coat gleamed from Tilly's endless brushing. He'd come a long way since his arrival at Silver Shoe, when he'd been a neglected horse in terrible condition.

Now he was a picture of health and everyone talked about how one day he could be a serious competition horse. He had very good conformation and looked like the sort of horse many top riders would choose. The only problem was that he didn't have the easiest of temperaments. Or rather, if anyone other than Tilly Redbrow was trying to ride him, he didn't always cooperate.

So if Magic really was going to aim for the top level, there was only one thing for it: Tilly would have to be the rider that took him there! Tilly thought about this as she painted his feet with hoof oil. When she'd finished she let him nuzzle her hair and neck. As his warm breath and whiskers tickled her ears she stroked his neck and gazed dreamily across the yard.

'Hey, Tilly, keeping busy?' came a
friendly voice.

Tilly was definitely busy, but that's how
she liked to be. She looked up and saw
Angela, Silver Shoe Farm's owner. Angela
was clearing out the club room, removing
stacks of aging storage boxes and bags of
old rosettes. They were beginning to pile
up in the yard.

11

'Hi, Angela. That's a lot of stuff!' said Tilly.

'I know. I've been meaning to tidy it for ages. Some of it goes back to when I was doing my first big eventing competitions. Brings back a few memories . . .'

'Those were the days, eh?' called Duncan, from across the yard.

Duncan was Angela's head boy. He and Angela had known each other for a long time. Tilly had always thought they'd make a nice couple, and her friends, Mia and Cally, had recently convinced themselves the pair were going out together. Tilly wasn't so sure. It would be nice if it were true but she knew better than to believe the rumours.

Duncan was doing some cleaning out of his own, forking bedding from the stable opposite Magic's. The stable's previous occupant, a small chestnut gelding called Archie, had moved with his owner to another county, so there was a space at Silver Shoe Farm. This was exciting as it didn't happen often. Tilly briefly wondered what kind of horse or pony would eventually fill it.

'Did you win any events?' she asked, watching Angela put down the last of the boxes.

'Oh, a few,' said Angela coyly.

'She won loads,' said Duncan. 'She was really good. She rode an amazing bay gelding called Pride and Joy. They had an incredible partnership.'

'Do you think you'll compete again? I'd love to see you.'

'I doubt it,' said Angela. 'I haven't competed for years. Unfortunately, Pride's competition days were cut short by injury. And after that, other rides just didn't feel the same. There was no other horse as special as him. I haven't seen him for a while. It makes me sad to see him retired. He's stabled in Long Bloxton, the other side of North Cosford, at his owners' place.'

As she said this her voice shook slightly. Tilly could see that thinking about Pride made Angela sad. She understood. The idea

of not seeing her favourite horse, Magic Spirit, was too distressing to think about.

'Long Bloxton's not far away,' said Tilly helpfully. 'You could still visit him, couldn't you?'

'Maybe . . . anyway, how's Magic doing?' said Angela, abruptly changing the subject.

'He's great, aren't you, boy?' said Tilly, as she reached up and patted Magic's shoulder.

'You've done a really good job with his coat. You're always so careful and thorough, Tilly. If every horse at Silver Shoe Farm was groomed by you, we'd have the best-kept stable yard in Cosford!'

As Tilly continued grooming, her mind drifted; jumping Magic Spirit over the biggest combination fence at Badminton Horse Trials, the lake where hundreds of

spectators were watching. She imagined all
the important people in her life standing in
the crowd cheering her on. Mia and Cally
and Becky were there. And Angela and
Duncan, and of course, her mum and dad
and younger brother, Adam. And then she
pictured Brook Ashton-Smith. He would
be at the front, cheering the loudest.

Not only had Silver Shoe Farm brought
Tilly and Magic Spirit together, it had led
her to find her long-lost brother, Brook,

thanks to the matching horsehair bracelets their real mum had given them just before she died. Brook was a talented rider and, like Tilly, his world revolved around horses.

Tilly and Brook didn't know much about their real mum, but one thing was certain, she'd given them both an instinct for horses. As Tilly stroked Magic's nose, she knew Brook also understood what it was like to have a special bond with a horse. He had Solo, his black thoroughbred.

Someone else who understood was Angela. Tilly thought about how upset she'd seemed when she talked about Pride and Joy. He obviously meant a lot to her. Why didn't she see him very often? Why was she so keen to change the subject?

'Mia!' she called, spotting her friend outside the tack room. 'We've got some investigating to do . . .'

Two

Tilly and Mia crouched over the boxes
that Angela had left in the yard and leafed
through the piles of papers and photographs.

'Look, there's Duncan with long hair
– how funny!'

'And look at this one. Everyone's
wearing fancy dress. Even Jack Fisher!'

The girls laughed. It was strange seeing
old pictures of the people they knew well.
Suddenly, in a box that was lying to the
side, separate from the others, Tilly found
what she wanted.

'There he is!'

She reached in and retrieved a wad of photographs and newspaper clippings, all bound together with a rubber band. Every image featured a huge bay gelding with a neatly plaited mane. He stood proudly, as though he knew he was a super star. He looked generous and loyal.

A newspaper clipping fell out of the pile. The headline read, 'Angela Fisher and Pride and Joy: Local Girl Wins Again'.

'That's him,' said Tilly. 'Pride and Joy, Angela's event horse. He sounds amazing.'

'I'd be scared jumping a horse that size,' said Mia.

'I bet Angela handled him though. I wish we could see them together.'

'No harm in suggesting it,' said Mia, as Angela came towards them, her curly red hair glowing in the sunlight.

'What are you guys up to?'

'Funny you should ask,' said Mia.

'We just found these photos of you and Pride,' said Tilly, with a little smile. 'We were wondering, since Long Bloxton isn't that far away, maybe you could take us to see him.'

'Oh,' said Angela, staring at the photographs of her and Pride. 'I haven't looked at these for ages.'

Tilly could see a sparkle of affection in Angela's eyes. She held her hands behind her back and twiddled with her horsehair bracelet hopefully.

'We could take a drive out there this afternoon, I suppose. I can tell you girls are going to pester me until I give in.'

Mia and Tilly glanced at each other and grinned. Tilly was glad. She wondered how Angela was feeling though. She couldn't wait to see Magic Spirit each morning, after not seeing him for the night. So it was hard to imagine what it would be like after not seeing him for months.

The drive out to Long Bloxton was fun. Tilly and Mia even managed to persuade Duncan to come with them. Along the way, Angela told the girls about her competition triumphs and how Pride had spent all his competing days at Silver Shoe Farm.

'He'll always be my favourite,' she explained. 'He took me to international honours – we did lots of eventing, not just in the UK, but also in Europe – France, Germany and Holland. We had plenty of wins. And then after his injury . . . well, it all came to an end. Pride's been retired for three years now. The vet said he would be sound enough to have an active life being hacked out by his owners, but he didn't think Pride could stand up to the extra rigours of eventing.'

The four-wheel drive pulled into the narrow lane that led up to the stable block. It wasn't as pretty as Silver Shoe Farm, but it was very grand, with twelve large stables around a square with a fountain in the middle. Pride and Joy was in the yard, tacked up and ready to be ridden. Tilly recognised him straightaway.

'Woah, he's huge!' said Mia.

'Must be at least 16.2hh,' said Tilly. She loved trying to guess the sizes of different ponies and horses. She was getting quite accurate too. She could see that Pride wasn't much bigger than Magic Spirit.

The moment Pride caught sight of Angela he quivered with excitement. She came towards him and showered him with kisses and hugs. Pride nuzzled Angela's

shoulder and rubbed his nose in her hair. They were both lost in their reunion.

Eventually, Mrs Mayhew, the owner,

22

came out and said hello. She greeted Angela with a hug and it wasn't long before they were talking about Pride's progress. The girls hovered about, admiring Pride and trying to listen in on the conversation.

"Pride's had three very easy years and the vet says he can't believe how well he's recovered. He really should be given another chance. He used to love competing and I know he must be bored just being here at the farm – it seems such a waste. He's definitely fit from all the hacking we've been doing, so he could easily be ready for the Cosford Horse Trials, with the right rider, of course."

Tilly and Mia smiled at each other.

'Maybe she *will* compete with him then?' said Tilly.

'I hope so.'

'Hope what?' A familiar voice interrupted them.

'Oh, hello, Duncan,' said Mia, blushing slightly.

'We were wondering whether Angela might compete with Pride,' said Tilly.

'Since they're such a good partnership.'

Duncan sighed. 'Good isn't the word. Angela's a gifted rider at the best of times, but the way she clicked with Pride, it's as though they were made for each other.'

'So will Angela take Pride to the Cosford Horse Trials?' asked Mia eagerly.

'If someone can convince her,' Duncan said, shrugging. 'I've tried, but it got me nowhere. For some reason, Angela thinks her competing days are over. She's always so busy training up other horses and trying to make good sales. She reckons there won't be time. It's such a pity. I know Pride's owners, the Mayhews, would be more than happy to see them compete together. Opportunities like this, top horse, professional rider, don't come along often. But Angela still seems reluctant.'

This was disappointing to hear. Tilly knew what a great horsewoman Angela was, because she'd watched her riding at the farm. What was stopping her? Tilly wondered. Was it just that she was too busy, or was there something else?

Three

On Sunday, Tilly missed her usual day of
riding and hanging out at Silver Shoe, but
she didn't mind. Brook was coming over
to the Redbrows' house for lunch. He'd
often done this since they'd realised they
were brother and sister and it was always
a fun occasion.

Tilly's mum was preparing her favourite
lunch: Greek salad with houmous and pitta
bread and that weird pink taramasalata
thing, which apparently was fish eggs,

although it tasted nice. Tilly was looking forward to showing off her vast collection of horsey stuff, including books, posters, computer games and magazines. Brook, of all people, appreciated it.

Brook arrived on time. Tilly greeted him at the door with a big hug, then they grinned as they spotted each other's horsehair bracelets. They would never forget how the bracelets had brought them together.

'Hello, Brook,' said Mr Redbrow.

'Lovely to see you again,' said Mrs Redbrow. 'Tilly won't stop talking about you – when she's not talking about Magic Spirit, that is!'

'Good to see you too,' said Brook with a smile. He handed Mrs Redbrow a bunch of flowers.

Tilly's little terrier, Scruff, tried to jump up and get them, but her brother, Adam, distracted Scruff with the television remote control.

'Don't give him that, Adam,' cried Mr Redbrow. 'You'll only encourage him, then one day you'll get back from football practice to find it chomped into little pieces. No more television!'

Mr Redbrow attempted to grab the

remote from Scruff, who ran off up the stairs. Mr Redbrow followed, knocking the telephone off the wall as he went. There was lots of crashing and banging. Adam whooped with laughter, while Mrs Redbrow sighed in despair.

Tilly smiled at Brook and rolled her eyes, as if to say 'Welcome to the Redbrow household'.

'You should see what it's like at Blade House,' he whispered. Blade House was where his adoptive family, the Ashton-Smiths had brought him up. Tilly thought it sounded very grand.

'My parents are really chaotic, especially my dad. He keeps parrots and lets them fly all round the house. We've got a massive Irish wolfhound too. And my mum's got this little Shetland. She brings her into the kitchen sometimes. She walks through the back door and watches us eat dinner!'

'Sounds great,' said Tilly. 'What about the other horses at Blade House?'

'Oh, they're not allowed in the house, thank goodness! There's Mum's chestnut geldings, Freddy and Mercury, Dad's black mare, Nessa, and everyone's favourite, old Mary-Ann, the skewbald. We've got thirty acres of grassland and an American-style barn where all the stables are under one roof. Last year my father had a sand arena put in, so I can train with Solo during the school holidays. You wouldn't believe the amount of sand that's needed to fill those things . . .'

Tilly tried to picture it.

'We still need to arrange for you to visit,' said Brook. 'What about the weekend after next? My parents have been going on about it since the last time they were up here.'

'Perfect,' said Tilly, as her mum nodded in approval. She was looking forward to it already.

They ate lunch in relative peace, once the Scruff/remote control incident had calmed down. When they'd finished and all the plates had been cleared away, Tilly and Brook went upstairs to her room.

'Your friend Becky wasn't kidding when she said your room was like Planet Pony! It amazes me every time I'm here,' Brook said, as he gazed around the walls and shelves.

Every inch of available space was crammed with horse-themed memorabilia.

There was a large photo collage above the bed, made up mainly of pictures of Magic Spirit, although some of the other Silver Shoe horses featured occasionally, including Bunny and Rosie, the ponies Tilly had learned to ride on.

There was the rosette Duncan and Red Admiral had won at the

Cosford Derby, thanks to Tilly's help. Duncan had given it to her as a gift. There was a framed photo of Tilly and Mia with Rosie. Tilly was growing too tall for her now and having to ride Magic Spirit more regularly (not that she minded). Next to that, there was a series of photos of Lucky Chance, the Silver Shoe foal, from when she was a tiny newborn to a weanling.

Tucked into the frame of the dressing table mirror were ticket stubs from Tilly's Christmas trip to the Olympia Horse Show, and the business card she'd been given by Samson's owner. Samson was an incredible stallion, who'd jumped higher than any other horse at the show. On the table itself, a gleaming silver trophy was displayed, which Tilly had won at her first ever Pony Club camp, for being the 'Most Improved Rider'.

Brook reached for a pile of magazines beside Tilly's bed. The one on top had a feature about the Burghley Horse Trials.

'I'm hoping I'll get to compete there one day,' he said.

'Wow!' said Tilly. 'Imagine. Brook Ashton-Smith, winner of the Burghley Horse Trials!'

'Who knows?' said Brook. 'Maybe . . . if everything carries on going well with Solo. So much depends on the confidence between the rider and the horse.'

'Hey, why don't we watch a DVD? I've got Burghley and Badminton and the Horse of the Year Show. I record them every year . . .'

'And watch them over and over again, I bet.'

Tilly blinked. 'How did you know?'

'I do the same.'

Tilly laughed, thinking, not for the first time, how funny it was that they were so similar when their backgrounds were so different. They were like brother and sister already.

They selected a few DVDs, the ones with all their favourite top riders, and took them down to the living room, where they sat back on two big bean bags and watched. As they did, they commented on the dos and don'ts of each rider's performance, occasionally pausing and rewinding. To Tilly's younger brother, Adam, this was highly annoying, but to them it was great fun. It was so good to share their enthusiasm.

As each combination of horse and rider rode around the cross-country, Tilly found herself thinking about Angela and Pride. Had they been as good as some of these

35

riders? Tilly thought about the look in Angela's eyes when she'd mentioned his retirement from competition, and the excitement in the air when they'd been reunited at the Long Bloxton stable.

Angela simply had to compete with him again. And Tilly had to find a way of convincing her.

Four

Later that evening Tilly went to Silver Shoe Farm to feed Magic Spirit. She swung open the gate and walked into the yard. Ahead of her, she could see the stables silhouetted against a vast orange-streaked sunset. Everything looked magical.

Tilly looked to see who else was around. There were a couple of pupils from Angela's classes, sitting outside the tack room cleaning their saddles, but apart from that it was quiet. As she wandered across the yard she heard some rustling in the empty stable opposite Magic's.

She crept over and peered through the door. Angela was in there, sitting on the ground with her legs stretched out and her back resting against the stable door. When she heard Tilly she looked up. She was misty-eyed, as though she'd been lost in her thoughts.

'Oh, hello.'

'Hi,' said Tilly. 'I didn't mean to disturb you. Are you okay?'

'Mmm . . . I was just thinking about Pride. It was so nice to see him again,' said Angela. 'This was his old stable. We were a great team once.'

'Duncan told me,' said Tilly. 'He said you won loads of events.'

Angela shrugged, a little embarrassed.

'A few,' she said. 'More importantly, we loved working together. I've spent all my life riding horses. I've worked with some good ones, some great ones, and quite a few difficult ones, but Pride is something beyond all that. He's special.'

Angela stood up and brushed the shavings off her jeans. Tilly wondered why, if Angela and Pride had such a special relationship, she didn't want to compete with him. It seemed like the perfect opportunity.

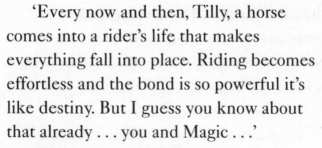

'Every now and then, Tilly, a horse comes into a rider's life that makes everything fall into place. Riding becomes effortless and the bond is so powerful it's like destiny. But I guess you know about that already . . . you and Magic . . .'

'Definitely,' said Tilly.

'That's why I want you two to work together. I can see you've got that special connection, and that connection makes anything possible.'

'Then you and Pride should compete at the Cosford Horse Trials,' said Tilly boldly.

Angela blinked, surprised. 'Oh I'm not sure I'd have time to train . . .'

This sounded like an excuse. Tilly could tell Angela wanted to, so why was she resisting?

'The truth is, Tilly,' she said eventually, 'it's been three years since I last competed. I'd love to do the Cosford Horse Trials with Pride but I don't know whether I've got it in me any more. I'd be really rusty, and nervous too. I lost quite a bit of confidence

when Pride injured himself at his last
competition – seeing him like that was
more shattering than any fall could ever be.
Besides, I don't want to look stupid and let
Pride down.'

'I bet you won't,' said Tilly. But she also
remembered what it was like at Pony Club
camp, where the girls in her group were all
more experienced than her and she was
worried about looking rubbish. She didn't,
of course. Her instructor was always full of
encouragement and praise. 'Anyway, how
will you know unless you try?' she added.
She felt a bit like her mum, or one of her
teachers at school.

'We'll see,'
said Angela.
There was
uncertainty in
her voice.

'Who knows,'
said Tilly,
persisting. 'You
might even win.'

'Oh, I doubt that.'

'But like you said,' said Tilly, her eyes twinkling, 'anything's possible.'

Tilly left Angela and headed to the long field to put feed out for Magic and the other horses.

As soon as Magic saw her at the fence he trotted towards her, confident and happy.

'Hello, boy,' she said affectionately, stroking his neck. 'Have you had a nice afternoon? I've been having lunch with Brook.' She always told Magic everything.

Magic nudged his nose into the crook of

Tilly's neck. She rubbed his cheek and made a sucking sound with her lips, which he really liked.

'The weekend after next,' she explained. 'I'm

going to his parents' house. Won't that be fun? I'll get to see Brook's family and all their animals.'

Magic nodded his head up and down as though he was taking it all in.

'Are you hungry?'

Tilly paused, seeing the excitement in Magic's eyes, as she rummaged in her pocket. 'I've got your favourite!'

She produced a couple of large carrots. He went straight for them, chomping and crunching.

'One day, you and I will compete in the Cosford Horse Trials,' she said, as he ate. 'Then Burghley and Badminton. And then maybe we'll compete in Europe. And then all over the world. We'll get one of those massive horse boxes, like all the top riders have. How cool would that be? Mia will come with us, and Cally. And Brook will be there too. I bet Solo will win everything.'

43

Tilly remembered what Brook had told her about his ambitions. She liked the idea of having a top eventer as a brother.

Tilly placed the other feeds well apart so the horses wouldn't fight, and returned to Magic. She stroked his nose as the last glimpse of sun slipped behind the trees. Spending time with him was the best thing ever. She wondered whether she'd ever get the chance to take him to top competitions. She still had a lot to learn, that was true. But she had a great teacher in Angela. She'd already learned so much from her.

She could learn so much more watching Angela compete at the Cosford Horse Trials. She hoped Angela would change her mind.

Five

On Tuesday morning, Tilly awoke to the sound of her mobile beeping. It was a text from Cally:

FANCY RIDING 2 THE LAKE AFTER SCHOOL?

MEET U AT SSF AT 5PM? X

Now that Cally was a student at Cavendish Hall, and kept her horse, Mr Fudge, stabled there, the girls had to grab every opportunity they could to get together.

Tilly replied immediately with a yes.

Suddenly her phoned beeped again. This time it was a text from Mia.

STOP PRESS. NEW HORSE STABLING AT SILVER SHOE.

NAME: PRIDE AND JOY!!! X

Tilly jumped. Did this mean Angela had decided to compete after all? She couldn't believe it!

School passed in a bit of a blur. Tilly couldn't stop thinking about Angela and Pride. When the last bell rang, she dashed to the school gates where she met Mia and her mum, and together they drove to Silver Shoe Farm.

As soon as they entered the yard, the girls went straight to the empty stable to see if Pride was in there. He wasn't and neither was Angela. This must be a good sign, thought Tilly. Maybe training was already underway. They were probably out together somewhere, doing jumps in the sand school or a lunging session.

The girls set about preparing their rides. Mia was taking Rosie. She wanted to ride her as much as she could this summer, because she was starting to get taller. Her parents had talked to Tilly's parents about selling Rosie in the autumn and finding Mia a horse.

Tilly was taking Magic Spirit. She gave him a light groom and brushed out his mane and tail. She checked his legs and feet carefully, which she always did before riding, just in case he had any small grazes or knocks from being out in the field. Angela said that regularly checking feet and legs was all part of good management.

By the time Tilly had tacked up, Mia was ready, and Cally and Mr Fudge were waiting in the yard. They had ridden over from Cavendish Hall.

'Hi, guys,' said Cally. 'Wow. You're

looking more confident with Magic every time I see you, Tilly. He's so well behaved with you.'

'Thanks. Mr Fudge is looking very handsome. I love his new bridle!'

'My parents sent it over from Dubai. I'm going to visit them soon.'

'You'll get to see some amazing horses out there,' said Mia. 'The Sheiks have loads of top racehorses in Dubai – thoroughbreds and Arabs. I read somewhere they even have camel racing!'

The three friends headed out of the farm gates and took the path that led through the fields and down to the lake. It was an hour long ride there and back, through open farmland. They took it slowly so they could chat and catch up on all the gossip. Tilly told Cally about Pride and Joy, and explained to her and Mia about her conversation with Angela.

'He's got such a lovely face,' said Tilly, describing Pride. 'Really gentle looking, but you can tell he's a performer. He's big and powerful, just oozing ability.'

'I'd love to see Angela competing on him,' said Mia. 'But the Cosford Horse Trials are only a month away. Do you think she'll be ready?'

'This is Angela we're talking about!' said Tilly reassuringly. 'She'll be fine. We just have to give her lots of encouragement

and make her feel confident, like she always does with us.'

When they reached the lake, the girls dismounted and let their horses munch on some grass. They tried skimming stones on the water but gave up when no one was successful. Instead they sat on a couple of old tree trunks on the banks of the lake holding Magic, Rosie and Mr Fudge's reins. As the sun started to get low in the sky, they knew it was time to get back to the stables.

Back at Silver Shoe, Tilly, Mia and Cally took a detour round to the sand school to see if they could spot Angela. There she was, working on Pride.

Duncan was adjusting fences for her. As well as some show jumps, he'd built some mock cross-country fences. There were a couple of oil drums too – one on its side, and another standing up – that were being used as arrow heads. Tilly knew this was so Angela and Pride could practise being accurate over very narrow fences. There were corner fences that Angela and Pride were jumping with ease, and angled rails too. The girls couldn't believe the tight angle Angela was approaching these fences on, but the rhythm never altered, and the pair of them looked as confident as if they'd won Badminton only yesterday.

Tilly had seen Angela ride before, when she was exercising the horses or demonstrating a technique to her students, but this was different. There was keenness and determination in her eyes. It was in Pride's eyes too. The connection between them was obvious.

'Brilliant!' said Mia.

'Well done,' said Cally.

Tilly remembered what Duncan had said about Angela and Pride being made for each other. Just then she felt a hand on her shoulder. It was Duncan.

'Impressive stuff, eh?' he said, nodding towards Pride and Angela.

'Definitely.'

'Just wanted to say thanks,' he whispered, smiling at Tilly.

'What for?'

'When Angela came to me yesterday and said she was bringing Pride over to get ready for the Cosford Horse Trials, I was amazed. She's said no to me so many times, I'd given up. And then she told me it was you who'd encouraged her to do it. I don't know what you said, but it worked. Not only are you a good little horse whisperer, but you're a bit of a people whisperer too!'

Six

Two weeks flew by, and Tilly was excited when the weekend came round. It was time for her trip to visit Brook's family at Blade House. She was going to ride Magic Spirit to Brook's boarding school, Cavendish Hall, and meet him there. Then they were getting a taxi to the station before catching the train.

Angela had offered to ride with her on the first part of the journey so she wouldn't have to be alone.

'It'll give Pride a chance to stretch out his legs,' she explained. 'It will be good for his fitness trotting up that steep hill to Cavendish Hall, and besides, I've always wanted to have a nose around there!'

They set off in the sunshine, casting tall shadows over the tarmac. Tilly felt very proud riding next to an impressive team like Angela and Pride, and pleased to be seen in public with Magic. She sat up tall and hoped people noticed what a fantastic horse he was.

'Do you feel ready for the Cosford Horse Trials?' she asked Angela. The event was only a couple of weeks away now so she knew Angela would be thinking about it.

'Well, so far I feel okay. Pride's legs look very good, and he feels great when I gallop him. Luckily he was in good condition when he arrived with us. It's me I'm worried about.'

'But you look so confident when you're training. We watched you jump the mock corner in the sand school and it was brilliant!'

'Cross-country I can handle, and the show-jumping round. It's the dressage test that causes problems. Nerves get to me. In previous competitions Pride has been a bit thrown by my jitters. He's always managed to cope with them – that's the kind of horse he is – but because this is the first event we've done together in ages, it's hard to know how he'll react.'

Tilly remembered her own experience of dressage at Pony Club camp. She knew what Angela meant. It was hard performing in front of people and keeping your concentration. There was so much to think about – it was difficult enough just remembering the test!

Magic and Pride walked through North Cosford, taking the quiet roads where there was less traffic. It was strange for Tilly and Angela, being so high up and peering into

58

everyone's front gardens. A few of the locals came out to the street to admire them.

When they left the town, they trotted up the hill that led to Cavendish Hall. This was a busier route, but car drivers were used to seeing horses on these country roads, and were very considerate. Angela acknowledged each driver by lifting her right hand, and signalling to them to say thank you for slowing down. She explained how important it was to always be courteous to drivers and other road users. Pride didn't seem bothered by the cars at all. Magic was a bit twitchy when a van went by, but other than that he coped well. Tilly thought again what a different horse he was now, compared to the one she'd rescued from the roadside all that time ago.

Finally they reached the large iron gates of the school. Brook was waiting for them on the gravel drive.

'Hi, guys,' he said, with an impressed smile. He stared at Pride. 'What a horse!'

'He's gorgeous, isn't he?' said Tilly. She

loved the fact that her new-found brother
was as obsessed by horses as she was. She
thought about the beautiful selection they
had between them: Solo, the handsome
black thoroughbred; Pride, the magnificent
event horse; and, of course, Magic Spirit,
the ultimate dream horse.

Tilly dismounted, just as a maroon car
pulled into the drive.

'I hear you're planning to tackle the
Cosford Horse Trials next month?' Brook

said to Angela. 'Tilly told me. I'd love to do it with Solo in a few years. Good luck.'

'Thanks,' said Angela. 'We're looking forward to it.'

'Well, looks like this is our cab. We'd better go or we'll miss our train.'

'Will you be okay leading Magic back home?' Tilly asked Angela.

'I'll be fine with these guys,' she replied.

Brook helped sort out Magic's reins and ran up the stirrups while Tilly said goodbye to him.

'Ready then? Have a nice trip!'

Magic snorted as if he was saying goodbye.

Tilly and Brook waved them off and climbed into the taxi. As the car pulled away, Tilly stared through the back window. She wanted one last glimpse of Magic. She hated being apart from him, even if it was just for a weekend. She watched as Angela got smaller and smaller in the distance, her red curly hair exploding beneath her riding hat, Magic following obediently behind her.

Then she looked forward. She couldn't wait to see what Blade House was like.

After a two hour train journey, Brook and Tilly took another taxi. They drove deep into the countryside.

'It's even quieter than Cosford,' said Tilly. 'There are hardly any houses!'

'It's mostly farmland,' said Brook. 'Our nearest neighbours are several miles away.'

Eventually, a large white building appeared among the patchwork of fields in the valley beneath them. It looked like a ranch, with a wide driveway sweeping towards it. Tilly could see a lake, an orchard, and a rectangle of concrete which she guessed was a tennis court. At the end of the large garden she could see an area of fenced-off grass, a square of sand and a small wooden building. This, she knew

straightaway, was the barn with the stables inside.

'Welcome to Blade House,' said Brook. 'I'll text my mum and tell her we're nearby. She's looking forward to seeing you again.'

Seven

As they walked up to the house, Brook's
parents came out.

'Lovely to have you here, Tilly,' said
Mrs Ashton-Smith, her arms held out.
'Goodness me! It shocks me every time I
see you together. It's clear you're related.
You've got the same eyes, the same
complexion, and the same smile!'

She couldn't stop staring at Tilly, and
then staring back at Brook. Tilly didn't
mind. She realised it must be pretty strange

to be looking at her son's long-lost sister.

They ate lunch around a long wooden table in the kitchen, which was bigger than the entire ground floor of the Redbrow house. Beneath their feet, the Ashton-Smiths' enormous Irish wolfhound, Doug, sniffed for scraps. He made Tilly's terrier, Scruff, seem like a little mouse.

There was potato salad and ham and fresh bread. Mr Ashton-Smith had a tray of pickles which he'd made himself. They were a bit unusual: turnip and anchovy, onion and grape, or nettle.

'Have a try, Tilly. They're my secret recipes.'

'You don't have to,' said Brook teasingly. 'No one likes Dad's pickles . . . except Doug!'

'So,' said Mrs Ashton-Smith, offering round a plate of hard-boiled eggs. 'It's no coincidence that Brook loves riding, since he's grown up around horses. What about you, Tilly? Are your family as horse-mad as us?'

'No,' said Tilly. 'My mum prefers ice-skating, my brother likes football and my dad thinks horses are a bit scary! They're all keen for me to ride, but they're not into it themselves.'

'I wonder where your talent comes from then?'

'It's obvious, isn't it?' said Brook. 'It's in

67

her blood. Maybe our birth mum was a horsewoman.'

'You'll have to find out more about her,' said Mr Ashton-Smith. 'Research your family tree, that sort of thing.'

Tilly and Brook glanced at each other. They were both thinking the same thing. The thought of finding out more about the mysterious woman in the photographs was very tantalising.

After lunch, Brook took Tilly down to meet the horses. There was a stunning barn,

housing ten wonderful stables, and for a
moment, Tilly felt a pang of envy. When
she saw the sand school at the opposite end
of the barn, she wished she could have
grown up there too. What would her life
have been like if she'd been adopted by the
Ashton-Smiths, been given her first pony
when she was five years old, and gone to
Cavendish Hall?

The envy didn't last long. Tilly quickly
remembered how much she loved her mum
and dad and Adam. She was a Redbrow
through and through. And of course, she
had Silver Shoe Farm, which was like a
second home to her. Above all, if her life
had been different, she might never have
met Magic Spirit, which didn't bear
thinking about.

There were four horses grazing in a
beautifully-manicured field, surrounded
by impeccable post and rail fencing. Brook
pointed them out. There were the two
geldings, Freddy and Mercury; the lively
young horse called Nessa; and the gentle

plodding mare, Mary-Ann. As soon as they noticed the visitors they came over.

'Solo loves coming back home,' said Brook. 'It's down-time after all the hard training we do at Cavendish Hall. I try and get home once a term, or sometimes Mum and Dad visit me, but Solo only comes back during the school holidays. Being home is the best. It's where we can both relax.'

'Do you think you'll keep Solo for a long time?' asked Tilly.

'I hope so. I want him to be the horse I get my first major competition success with.'

'I can just imagine it . . .'

'And you too, Tilly. With a horse like Magic, who knows what you'll achieve?'

'Anything's possible,' she said. 'Maybe we could be the first top brother and sister team.'

'Absolutely,' said Brook.

'Are you going to the Cosford Horse Trials in a few weeks' time?' said Tilly. 'To see Angela and Pride compete? It's going to be a really exciting day.'

'Definitely,' said Brook. 'I heard some of the stable lads at Cavendish Hall talking about them. Horses like that get everyone interested.'

Eight

Brook and Tilly arrived back in North
Cosford on Sunday evening.

'Thanks for a great weekend,' said Tilly,
as the cab dropped her off. 'I really like your
mum and dad. They're fun.'

'No problem. Next time we get
together, we'll see what we can find out
about our family tree, shall we?'

'Yes. I'd love to know more about our
mum. And her horse.'

'Me too,' said Brook. 'Well, bye then.'

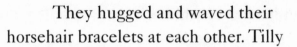

They hugged and waved their
horsehair bracelets at each other. Tilly
turned and went to her
front door. She could
hear Scruff barking
and Adam laughing.
The familiar sounds
were comforting. She
realised she was looking forward to seeing
her own family.

It wasn't long, however, before Tilly
was out again. Mr Redbrow took her over
to Silver Shoe so she could check on Magic.
Magic was pleased to see her, and especially
pleased to eat the carrot treat she'd brought
him.

'Come on, boy. Let's get you out to
graze before night fall.'

They walked past the sand school,
where Angela and Pride were practising the
dressage test. Duncan was watching from
the fence. Naturally, Tilly was interested,
but it was Magic who insisted on stopping
for a while. It was as if he was thinking

about having a try himself.

'Hi, Tilly,' said Duncan.

'Hiya, how's training going?'

'As you can see, Angela's still at it. She's such a perfectionist. She wants to make sure she's practised every move and gone over every kind of jump possible. Yesterday, we drove out to Maynard's Farm, where they've got a cross-country course set up. We worked on steps, 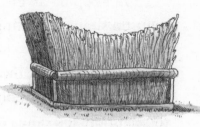 coffins, ditches, drop logs and triple brushes. Today it's been all about precision – the half-pass and the trot to halt.'

'Pride looks like he knows what he's doing.'

'Oh yes,' laughed Duncan. 'Pride is ready for anything. It's Angela who wants the practice. She keeps saying she's forgotten how to do things. She hasn't of course, it's just her worrying. She's making herself ride without stirrups to improve her seat and balance. And she's also been riding with a stick behind her back to make herself sit up really tall.'

'Won't she over-train?'

'I'm keeping an eye on things. We don't want to wear Pride out before his big day but it's always best to be over-prepared in eventing. That way, the challenges of the event itself will be well within the horse's capabilities. You don't want to get there and find that you have to put your horse over fences that are bigger than anything he's ever jumped before.'

'That makes sense,' said Tilly.

'Quality not quantity. That's what counts in training,' said Duncan.

Tilly nodded. She always listened to the advice of experienced riders like Duncan and Angela. She knew there was so much she could learn from them. She stroked Magic's mane and imagined it was him in the sand school, preparing for his first competition.

What would it be like, she wondered, if it was the pair of them competing at the Cosford Horse Trials? She thought about how she would feel in the build up to the competition: excitement, nerves, determination. She pictured herself waking up on the day of competition, getting dressed in her smart riding jacket and breeches, plaiting Magic's mane (she was famed for her neat plaits!), sorting out his tack, chatting to other riders, then finally, getting her number and tying it around her waist.

Tilly felt excited just thinking about it.

'Tilly? Tilly?'

A few minutes later Angela's voice jolted her back to reality.

'Are you with us or are you lost on Planet Pony?'

'Uh, yes, sorry, I was in a day dream.'

Angela smiled.

'Could you help me move some of the horses into the long field? We'll take Magic and Pride with us. I think Pride has had enough practice today, and I certainly have!'

'Sure,' said Tilly.

As they walked, horses at their sides, Angela chatted about the travel arrangements for the competition in two weeks' time. Her quick talk made her seem nervous. At first Tilly wondered what it had to do with her, then Angela stopped and suddenly looked very serious.

'Tilly, I was hoping, if you're available . . . that you might want to groom for me at the competition.'

Tilly gasped, delighted.

'I'd love to!'

'Great. I'm so glad. This is a really important competition for me and I guess I have you to thank. It was your enthusiasm

78

that convinced me to go for it, so it would mean a lot if you could be part of the day too.'

Tilly clapped her hands together excitedly. Magic, sensing her happiness, did a little shuffle from side to side.

'Besides,' said Angela. 'You're one of the most conscientious grooms at Silver Shoe Farm. You always take extra care and your plaits are perfect. Even if we don't win, Pride will be one of the neatest, shiniest horses on show!'

Tilly was thrilled – being asked to groom for Angela felt like the next best thing to actually competing. She would get to be part of the experience. Not just a spectator but a member of the team. It was such an honour.

'It'll be an early start,' warned Angela. 'But I know you won't mind that.'

Tilly knew she'd stay up all night if she had to.

'It's also a good opportunity for you to experience the ins and outs of the eventing scene, get used to how everything happens, learn the ropes. A young rider's first big event can be quite daunting, but if they've been to plenty of competitions as a groom beforehand it really helps. I did it when I was your age. So did Duncan. He used to

80

groom for Cavendish Hall!'

Tilly giggled. They approached the
long field. Lucky Chance and her mum,
Lulabelle, were grazing near the trees. At
the far end, Red Admiral was letting off

some steam, galloping from one fence to
another. He looked free and happy, with
his mane and tail fluttering in the wind.

'I bet you'd like to join him,' said Tilly,
smiling at Magic.

Pride snorted and let out a whinny.

'You too, boy,' said Angela.

81

Suddenly, Tilly felt like everything was coming together. There was nothing she liked better in the world than being at Silver Shoe Farm, surrounded by her favourite horses.

Nine

On the day of the competition, Tilly was up before her alarm, rehearsing all the things she had to do for Pride and Angela in her head. By the time her mum dropped her off at Silver Shoe, she'd been through the whole day about ten times!

'Good morning, Tilly,' said Angela. 'Pride is in his stable. If you groom and plait him here, then he can have a general buff-up once we get to the event. Here's some thread to match his mane. He had it pulled yesterday, so it should be fairly easy. Is that okay? He's pretty clean because he had a complete shampoo yesterday as well.'

'Perfect,' said Tilly.

She took the thread and went straight to Pride's stable. The sun was just beginning to rise over the stables. Tilly tied Pride in the washbox, where there was plenty of light, and checked him over. He looked incredibly fit. He was on top form, as good as any of the event horses she'd seen on television.

'You're going to make Angela proud. I just know it,' she whispered, as she ran her hands over his legs. They were all fine. 'Now I hope you don't mind, boy, but I'm only going to give you a small hay-net this morning while I muck out.'

Tilly knew when they returned that evening, everyone would be exhausted. The last thing they'd want to do was muck out. This way, it would all be ready for Pride's return. She hoped Pride wouldn't mind only having a small amount to eat this morning. Angela had explained that she shouldn't give him much hay, if any. It was important Pride didn't have bulk in his stomach before competing.

Once the stable was done, Tilly gave Pride's coat a brush. Then she sponged his eyes, nose and dock and used a stable rubber to polish and remove the last traces

of dust from his body. It was satisfying to
see such a splendid shine appear across his
coat. She wanted him to look his very best
in front of the judges.

Finally, it was time for Tilly's favourite
bit – plaiting.

She dampened Pride's mane with a wet
brush and divided it into sections then,
starting from behind the ears, she plaited all
the way down. She secured each plait with
the thread.

Tilly then moved to Pride's rear,
brushed his tail and put a tail bandage on it.
She kept the stray hairs. She knew exactly
what she'd do with those. She'd made
horsehair bracelets for many of her friends,
from the tail hairs of horses that were
special to them. Angela definitely deserved
one from Pride.

Just then, Duncan called her.

'Wow! You've done a great job! Are you
nearly finished?' He stopped suddenly. 'Oh,
I nearly forgot, I haven't checked his stud
holes – they'll need cleaning out so the

studs screw in easily.'

'I wondered what those two holes in each shoe were for,' said Tilly.

'Studs are essential in eventing to stop the horses from slipping,' Duncan explained. 'Now let's get Pride into the lorry. I'll help you get his travel boots and blanket on.'

'Thanks,' Tilly said. She stuffed the tail hairs into her jeans pocket, deciding she would make the bracelet during the journey. She wanted to be able to give it to Angela before she started competing.

Tilly loved the atmosphere and general bustle of competitions. This one was no different. She climbed out of Angela's lorry and soaked it up.

It was as if the estate of Cosford House, where the event was being held, had been hijacked by horses for the day. The park was crammed with some unbelievable horse boxes, but hardly any trailers. The house itself – a big grey mansion – was being used as a collection point for competition times and numbers.

Angela dropped the ramp of the lorry and she, Tilly and Duncan checked Pride. Tilly thought he looked amazingly relaxed considering he hadn't been to a competition for three years.

'He's done it a million times before,' said Duncan, shrugging. 'It's second nature to him.'

Tilly was relieved. She knew that if Pride remained calm and content, it would help Angela control her nerves.

Angela had every detail of the day planned out. She waved her schedule, which was typed on a

sheet of paper, at Duncan.

'I told you she was a perfectionist,' he joked, giving Tilly a nudge.

'Ha ha,' said Angela sarcastically. She wasn't in a joking mood. 'I need to pick up my number and then walk the cross-country course.'

'I'll come with you if you like,' said Duncan. 'I'll help you work out the best way to jump.'

'Thanks. While we're doing that, maybe you could get Pride ready for the dressage test, Tilly. It would be great if you could give his coat a final polish before tacking up.'

'Okay,' said Tilly.

This was a big responsibility. She was very flattered that Angela trusted her, but a little bit nervous too.

'You'll be fine,' said Duncan, with a wink. 'Before I go, I'll just open the partition for you to give you a bit more room. And when we're back from walking the cross-country I'll put his studs in for you.'

Tilly smiled, pleased that Duncan had faith in her too. She fetched everything she needed and got to work. Pride stood very tall and confident, as though he was psyching himself up for the event.

Tilly gave him a thorough polish with a stable brush and applied some fly repellent. She checked his saddle, bridle, stirrups and girth and then began tacking up.

Some people walked past the lorry, looking up the ramp at Pride. 'What a wonderful-looking horse,' Tilly heard someone remark. She felt proud to be responsible for such an impressive ride.

'Look at you, boy. You're getting all the attention. Go well for Angela, won't you? This means so much to her.'

Pride looked at her with his dark, soulful eyes then he leaned towards her and nabbed one of her plaits in his teeth.

'Hey! They're not for chewing!' she said, releasing it from his grip. 'I hope that's your way of saying 'Yes, Tilly, I'll do whatever you say'. Look, here come Brook,

90

Mia and Cally.'

Tilly waved at them. Brook and Cally had arrived together on the Cavendish Hall school bus. Mia had met them at the entrance.

'Hi, Tilly. Hello, Pride,' said Brook.

'We saw him from a distance and said, 'Wow, that horse looks amazing, then we realised *you* were tacking him up,' said Cally. 'You look like a pro!'

'Thanks. I hope I've done everything properly.'

'Looks all right to me,' said Brook. 'I'll check if you like.'

Brook tested each of the buckles and adjusted the angle of the saddle slightly.

'There we go. Perfect. Maybe you could groom for me when I compete with Solo? He's always really calm when you're around.'

'Definitely,' said Tilly, remembering what Angela had said about getting lots of experience in competitions and shows.

Ten

Angela was impressed with Tilly's grooming and asked her to be on hand for the rest of the competition. Tilly liked feeling useful. She reached into her pocket and gave Angela the bracelet she had made from the tail hairs she'd collected when grooming Pride.

'How lovely! Thanks, Tilly,' said Angela. 'Your bracelet certainly helped Duncan and Red Admiral – let's hope it'll do the same for me!'

She showed the bracelet off to Duncan, Brook and Cally. In return they showed her their bracelets. Duncan had Red Admiral's tail hairs, Brook had Solo's, and Cally had Rosie's.

'It's quite a collection we've got between us,' said Brook.

'I haven't got one,' said Mia, pouting slightly.

'Don't worry,' said Tilly, smiling at her. 'I'm sure I'll make you one eventually.'

'Right,' said Angela, as she checked the time on her watch. 'Not long to go now. I'd better start getting changed.'

Angela went into the small living area of her lorry and came out a few minutes later dressed immaculately in her top hat and tails. Tilly thought she looked wonderful. She'd seen pictures of Angela at competitions before, but had never seen her wearing this outfit for real.

Then it was time for Angela to begin her special pre-competing routine. She wanted to get on Pride at least forty minutes before the dressage test.

'Normally I'd have given him just half an hour, but because he hasn't competed for a while, I want to make sure he's calm,' she explained to Tilly. 'This way we can take our time, and I can canter him so he's relaxed and focused, and get rid of any excess energy.'

Once mounted, Tilly thought Angela and Pride looked the picture of elegance. Within five minutes of Angela riding him, Pride started to settle and she began to warm him up.

Just twenty minutes later, Pride was soft, submissive and responding to every command Angela gave, so they moved into a walk. Then, with a little over five minutes to go, Tilly removed Pride's exercise boots and gave him one final polish. Angela picked up the reins, gave a little nudge with her legs, and worked Pride for a few more minutes before heading straight into the dressage arena.

Tilly stood beside Duncan and watched.

'Keep it together,' whispered Duncan. He held tight to his own horsehair bracelet, hoping it would bring Angela luck.

Angela worked through the test with careful concentration. To Tilly, it looked perfect, but Duncan told her there were a few tiny mistakes. Tilly stood, gaping, amazed to see how a big horse like Pride could look so light and graceful. And he certainly looked sleek after all that grooming.

Tilly could see from the smile on Angela's face that she was delighted with Pride's performance. She walked alongside an elated Angela back to the lorry, where

she had to make a quick change of tack for
the jumping. She changed the saddle over,
put on some special jumping boots, and
added a martingale bridle. Then Tilly went
to the warm-up area with Duncan to watch
Angela and Pride do a few practice jumps.
As Pride was jumping so well outside,
Angela entered the ring before her time.

'Fingers crossed,' said Duncan.

'The important thing here,' said Brook,
'is to let the horse know he's now in 'jump
mode'. Watch how Angela rides Pride
forward. She's asking him to be brisk and
positive, letting him know that it's time for
action.'

They headed for the first jump with
keenness and confidence. Angela looked a
lot more relaxed and in her element, as if
she was back at Silver Shoe Farm. Tilly
could see the enjoyment return to her face.
This would surely help her.

Pride used all of his power and strength
to sail over the fences. Some of them looked
enormous but he wasn't daunted.

In lessons, Angela always told Tilly to approach fences straight and to maintain balance. She also discouraged too much rider interference. She believed it was important to let the horse work the jump out for himself. Now Tilly could see all of this advice coming together. Her straightness, rhythm and relaxed hands produced a perfect round. Everyone cheered as they made the transition down to a walk and left the ring.

'Fantastic!'

'Well done!'

Angela dismounted and received a big hug from Duncan. Cally and Mia raised their eyebrows and nudged each other. Meanwhile Tilly knew she had grooming responsibilities. She held Pride while everyone praised him, then led him back to the lorry for another change of gear. They had an hour and a half until the cross-country round, so she gave Pride some water and undid his plaits. She didn't change the saddle this time, but gave him a different bit – a gag – so he wouldn't be able to pull quite as strongly.

An hour and a half later, Angela and Pride were back together and ready to go. Angela had changed into her lucky lemon-yellow polo shirt and was wearing a body protector and champion crash helmet.

'Wait!' Tilly exclaimed suddenly, just as Angela was slipping her competition number into her bib. 'Let me write my lucky number on the back!' She scribbled down the number '7' and passed it back to Angela. 'Now you have that *and* Pride's horsehair bracelet – twice the luck.'

'Thanks, Tilly – as if you haven't done enough today already!' said Angela, as she double-checked the girth was tight enough before mounting.

'What's your master plan for this bit?' asked Brook. Now that he'd seen Angela perform he was keen to pick up tips.

'Adaptability is vital,' she explained. 'You need to be able to think on your feet – or should I say hooves! Cross-country can throw up so many surprises – slippery ground, awkward jumps. It's what makes it exciting, but the safety of you and your horse always needs to be a top consideration. And going flat out to get inside the time doesn't necessarily mean a win.'

Tilly also listened, taking it all in. One day she hoped Angela's advice would be echoing in her head as she prepared for the start of her own cross-country round with Magic Spirit.

'Time to go,' said Duncan.

With his assistance, Angela swung her leg over. She adjusted her position in the saddle, picked up the reins and moved away. The others wished her luck then went to find a good viewing spot where they could see lots of fences.

They ended up beside a quiet wooded area near a palisade with a massive ditch in front of it. It looked big enough to get a car through. They looked out for Angela and Pride but it was a tense wait. There was a nervous hush in the air. Tilly couldn't help running a few disasters through her mind. What if Pride had refused the first jump?

What if Angela's nerves had returned? What if they'd fallen?

Suddenly, in a blur of lemon-yellow and bay, legs thundering over the grass, Angela and Pride passed. They leapt over the ditch and palisade as if they were little more than a cross pole, then they were gone.

Tilly blinked, mesmerised.

'Well, that was quick!'

'But highly impressive,' said Brook. 'I reckon they've nailed it.'

They watched another competitor. He had a bit of a wobble as his chestnut gelding stretched over the wide log then splashed into the water. It was a tricky obstacle.

It was soon time to head to the last jump. They wanted to catch Angela as she came in. They made it with only a minute to spare. Angela appeared on the finishing straight. Her breeches and polo shirt were splashed with mud, but Tilly guessed that was a good thing – it meant she'd ridden boldly and not allowed her nerves to get the better of her.

It seemed as though she was thinking about nothing but the finish ahead of her, eyes fixed in front, body pressed forward, Pride's legs pounding beneath her. But as soon as she crossed the line and began to slow, she relaxed. An enormous, relieved smile spread across her face. She leaned forward and kissed Pride's neck.

The gang gathered round.

'What a ride!' said Duncan.

'That was awesome!' said Brook.

Angela was so giddy with happiness, she was barely aware of the compliments people were giving her. She did manage to catch Tilly's eye, however, with a look that seemed to say 'this is all thanks to you'. Tilly felt immensely proud.

The judges announced Angela's time. It was just inside.

'Could be another Angela-Pride win,' said Duncan hopefully. 'No one else has managed it so far . . .'

'Win or lose, I don't care,' said Angela, grinning. 'The most important thing is that was the best fun I've had in ages! I only wonder why it took me so long? I love it!'

They all huddled together to share in Angela's thrill – everyone except Tilly, who still had grooming duties to perform.

'It's all work, work, work!' she sighed,

watching the others hopping up and down with excitement.

But she didn't really mind. In the time it took for Tilly to get Pride's tack off and his head collar on, Duncan arrived to help.

'That's it, Tilly, use plenty of water,' he advised. 'It's important to get him cool as quickly as possible. Great. Now scrape the excess water off with the sweat scraper.'

Duncan threw a sweat rug over Pride, while Tilly offered him a refreshing bucket of water.

'Now,' Duncan continued, 'why don't you take him for a walk until he stops puffing? And remember not to let him eat until his breathing is back to normal, then he can have some grass.'

'It's amazing how much I still have to learn,' said Tilly.

'You'll find you never stop learning with horses,' replied Duncan, smiling.

'Pride and Joy,' Tilly whispered, as she walked with him through the grounds. 'Pride and Joy. Well, you've certainly lived up to your name.'

Pippa's Top Tips

Always check your horse's legs and feet carefully before riding in case they have any small grazes or knocks from being out in the field. Regular checking of legs and feet is all part of good management.

When riding on the road, you should always be courteous to drivers and other road users. Raise your right hand to signal 'thank you', or nod your head politely to cars as they slow down for you.

Never tie your horse up directly to the bit, always use a head collar, because you risk the bit cutting into their mouth if they pull away.

It's best to be over-prepared in eventing so you can be sure that the challenges of the event itself will be well within the horse's capabilities.

As part of preparation for an event, why not practise improving your seat and balance by riding without stirrups?

Grooming for more experienced riders at events is a great opportunity to learn the ropes and get a feel for the ins and outs of the eventing scene.

The morning before a competition, give your horse a smaller hay-net than usual. They shouldn't have too much bulk in their stomachs before competing.

Studs are essential in eventing to stop the horses from slipping. Make sure the stud holes in your horse's shoes are cleaned out properly so that the studs screw in easily.

Get on your horse at least half an hour before the start of your event. This will help get rid of any excess energy, and ensure your horse is relaxed and focused before the real work starts.

When the event is over, ensure your horse gets plenty of water – it's important to cool him down as quickly as possible. But remember not to let him eat until his breathing has returned to normal.

For more about Tilly and Silver Shoe Farm –
including pony tips, quizzes and everything
you ever wanted to know about horses –
visit www.tillysponytails.co.uk